Acknowledgments

Literacy Volunteers of New York City gratefully acknowledges the generous support of the following foundations and corporations that made the publication of WRITERS' VOICES and NEW WRITERS' VOICES possible: An anonymous foundation; The Vincent Astor Foundation; Exxon Corporation; Knight Foundation; Scripps Howard Foundation; Uris Brothers Foundation and H.W. Wilson Foundation.

We deeply appreciate the contributions of the following suppliers: Cam Steel Die Rule Works Inc. (steel cutting die for display); Canadian Pacific Forest Products, Ltd. (text stock); Creative Graphics, Inc. (text typesetting); Westvāco Corporation (cover stock); MCUSA (display header); Delta Corrugated Container (corrugated display); Stevenson Photo Color Company (cover color separations); and Coral Graphics Services, Inc. (cover printing); R.R. Donnelley & Sons Company (text printing and binding).

For their guidance, support and hard work, we are indebted to the LVNYC Board of Directors' Publishing Committee: James E. Galton, Marvel Comics Ltd.; Virginia Barber, Virginia Barber Literary Agency, Inc.; Doris Bass, Scholastic, Inc.; Jeff Brown; Jerry Butler, William Morrow & Co., Inc.; George P. Davidson, Ballantine Books; Joy M. Gannon, St. Martin's Press; Walter Kiechel, *Fortune*; Geraldine E. Rhoads; Virginia Rice, Reader's Digest; Martin

Singerman, News America Publishing, Inc.; James L. Stanko, James Money Management, Inc. and F. Robert Stein, Pryor, Cashman, Sherman & Flynn.

Thanks also to George Davidson, Caron Harris and Steve Palmer of Ballantine Books for producing this book; Alison Mitchell for her thoughtful copyediting and suggestions and to Pam Johnson and Allegra D'Adamo for their dedicated work on this project.

We would like to thank the following people and institutions for their assistance with this project: Dale Marlin; ILLINOIS: Robert Spellman, Sheridan Correctional Center; MASSACHUSETTS: Pat Mew, Hampshire County House of Correction; MINNESOTA: Roz Gilbert, Minnesota Correctional Facility; NEW YORK: C. Nealon, Vonda Caccese, Washington Correctional Facility; VIRGINIA: Dr. Hillal Gill, Virginia Department of Correctional Education; Roy Haliburton and Jerri Robertson, Hanover Learning Center; George Erps, Appalachian Correctional Unit; Dana Rhodenizer and David McKnight, Staunton Correctional Center; Sharon Trimmer, Bon Air Learning Center; VERMONT: Susan Mahler, Woodstock Correctional Center; WISCONSIN: Tracy Bredeson, Waupun Department of Correction.

For their hard work and enthusiastic participation, we would like to thank our student authors.

Our thanks to Paul Davis Studio and Myrna Davis, Paul Davis, Lisa Mazur, Chalkley Calderwood and Alex Ginns for their inspired design of the covers of these books. Thanks also to Jules Perlmutter for his sensitive design of the interior of this book.

CONTENTS

Bars Coming Near

Mark W. Peterson (*Minnesota*)

Cold steel against warm skin
Lonely back seat
A bird in a cage
Bars coming near.

Short ride
Questions never end
Orange suit to wear
Bars coming near.

Long dark hallway
Steel door closes
Click of the key
Bars here.

Let Go

Lynn K. (*Virginia*)

It's going to be a difficult time.
You just can't change your feelings at one toss
    of a dime.
Ever since I met him, my whole being has been
    rocked to and fro.
To regain some balance, I have to let go.

It's been an eternity since he held me.
It's been forever since we've seen each other.
I tried to carry on
For, really, I could not see.
Now that I am starting to understand and
    know,
I realize it's long past time to let go.

Our Time Apart

Brandon K. Daniels (*Virginia*)

I understand and realize how difficult it is for you during our time of separation because I, too, am suffering. I also experience the loneliness at night and the anger at life because of our situation.

I'm sorry for the times I'm not there to share your happiness or soothe your wounds. I'm sorry for the times on the phone when I make small talk and all we really need is a hug. But there is one thing I am not sorry for, and that is loving you.

Our time apart is small when compared to a lifetime of togetherness. If we are strong, our feelings will not fade with time. Rather, they will grow stronger with each passing day.

Stuff

Richard P. Tomaskowicz (*Massachusetts*)

I like stuff. "Stuff" is my word for a commodity, knick-knack, souvenir or what have you. I enjoy fleamarkets, tag sales and auctions. There are a number of good shops in the area, too.

I started collecting to have things to work on in my shop. I always said that when I had enough stuff, I would have a big tag sale, but that never seems to happen. I just keep getting more and more stuff. I have run out of rooms to decorate and am convinced I need a bigger house.

I like stuff. I will see what looks like a piece of junk, but something about its character will spark an idea and I will have to have it. When it comes out of my shop, it is the same thing, only different.

It gives me a sense of identity to have my stuff my way. I like stuff. My problem is getting rid of it. Each piece has a place, a story behind it and a reason for being. I don't know why, I just like stuff.

Using Prison Time in a Positive Way

Johnny E. Underwood (*Virginia*)

Being in prison was hard for me at first. I couldn't read, but I wanted to read my own mail. I felt helpless knowing that I had to share my mail. At 39, I decided that I wanted to do something about this—I signed up for school.

While waiting for a school pass, I drew cartoon characters and flowers on envelopes. To make ends meet and occupy my time, I also did matchstick crafts making jewelry boxes and statues.

I finally received my pass for school. I attend classes every morning. Two years have passed and things are a lot better. I no longer have to share my mail. I can read!

I still do my cartoon characters, flowers and crafts. But learning to read has been the key to my prison life because it's what helps me use my time in a positive way.

The Thieving Raccoon

Michael Shawn Wright (*Virginia*)

Once, a long time ago, in the deepest woods farther than you can imagine, there lived an old doctor in a little old house under a big oak tree. It was December, the dead center of winter.

The past summer had not been one of the doctor's better ones. First, he had not received a letter from his children the whole year. He was really worried about them. Even though they were grown up, he still worried about them. And second, his garden had not produced one single vegetable. After all the plowing he had done with his tractor, and all the planting and fertilization, he still did not get one vegetable. And since he had no vegetables, he had nothing to can for the winter.

On this particular day, the doctor had run out of food and he was hungry. He was still trying to explain to himself what had gone wrong with his garden that summer. Finally, the doctor got so hungry that he went outside to look for food.

It was very cold out and he was frozen.

Suddenly, he noticed some tiny footprints in the snow. He decided to follow them. They led to the place where he had planted his garden last summer.

In the corner of the garden, he saw a hole in the ground. He went over to take a better look. Peering inside, he saw a black and gray raccoon sitting there, eating some carrots. And spread out all around him were the vegetables from the garden. It was an even bigger surprise when the doctor saw a pile of letters among the vegetables. The raccoon had stolen the stuff!

The old doctor went and got his tractor. He dug around the hole to make the opening larger. He went in and brought out the vegetables, the letters and the raccoon.

The doctor took everything in the house. And he and the raccoon had a real home-cooked supper.

The Old Wooden Church

Lewis Lee Jones (*Virginia*)

As I went down an old dirt road,
I saw in front of me an old, old wooden church.
When I got near, I took a good long look.
The paint was peeling, the steeple half gone.
In the last rays of sunset, I walked up the steps
and through its wide-open door.
Many Sundays this landmark had faced but
there would be no more.
I walked in. There stood an old wooden pulpit,
still blessed with grace.
Then I placed a bench in its once proper space.
There on the floor lay an old wooden fan by a
battered old hymnal left by some Christian
hand.
I savored each step where voices once sang.
Then I walked outside through the tall grass
and knelt by a tombstone, old, rotten and
gray.
The words of a song I heard quietly in my
head.
I began to pray.
Then I turned and went on with spiritual love.
God had visited me at that old wooden church.

Twelve Years

Daniel Abrego (*Illinois*)

When I stood in front of the judge and heard the word "guilty" come out of his mouth, I couldn't believe that something that had happened in a couple of seconds was going to cost me the next 12 years of my life. It didn't seem fair. I felt like shouting and telling him he was making a big mistake. I wanted to cry.

I turned and saw my family and friends and the grief in their eyes. When I saw the tears rolling down my mother's face, I wished I could die. I turned to look at the judge and wanted to give him a piece of my mind but that feeling was drowned out by the anger inside me. I blamed him for the tears, the sadness and everything that was happening.

When the officers put me on the bus, I felt like nothing was of importance anymore. I didn't care about anything that could happen in my world, the world that was once called my life. I felt that for the next 12 years, it would be as if I were dead. In a way, that's what happened. They killed me; they took my life away.

On the bus, all I could hear were the sirens of the police cars that escorted us to the penitentiary. When I saw the officers holding their weapons in their hands, I knew that this was big time. I was on my way to a place where there is no love, no friends, no trust. A place where only the strong survive. Did I have what it takes? Was I strong enough to survive?

Nobody on the bus was speaking. I guess they were all as afraid as I was. I can still see the houses going by. I never thought I would appreciate the things that life is made up of so much. The grass looked so green, the trees were so beautiful. I saw some children playing with one another. I could almost hear their laughter—the laughter I wouldn't hear again for such a long time.

In Search of
the Perfect World

Clarence Johnson (*Virginia*)

If you could dream of a perfect world, what kind of world would it be? And if you had the power to create the perfect world, how would you go about creating it?

You could start by having a great leader like Dr. Martin Luther King, Jr., who had the perfect dream. "I have a dream," King said. "I have a dream that one day this nation will rise up and live out the true meaning of its creed: that all men are created equal."

With a dream like that, you could have the perfect world. Picture all the people in the world having love for one another. Picture the world without racial problems.

Can you imagine a world without hate, nuclear weapons, disease and, above all, a world without drugs? And can you picture a world with no wars, no hunger, and peace among all the nations? And picture a world without pollution, and the same educational opportunities in every nation.

This is the perfect world I would like to live in.

My Blues

Anthony Blevins (*Virginia*)

Searchin' for peace, I travel alone
Down a long, long, lonely road.
Only my life, my life I own.
Man of the sixties,
The nineties I roam
Rebelling against things I feel wrong.
One day I'll be free
And free I do belong.
Till then, keep walkin' on,
Holes in my pockets,
Now carrying on
Barefoot, no shoes.
Trapped in the nineties
Reason for my blues.
Late-born hippie
Headed back to my time.
Gotta get there quick,
Can't waste no time.
Travelin' down this long narrow road,
Never wanta stop singing the blues.

Holding On

John Lefas (*Massachusetts*)

The booming surf could be heard but not seen in the black, velvet night. Not a star nor the moon were about to light my way upon the heaving swell. I was at the mercy of the raging seas, tossed all around like a leaf in autumn. Hold on, hold on . . . to a line . . . to a ship's timber . . . to a hope . . . to a life.

Hunger ate at me, fatigue wracked my bones and memories haunted me. Still I held and hoped. The alternate hissing and rumbling of the breaking rollers was closer. Would I be broken on the reef or mercifully set on a beach? Pondering my fate, I turned to the dark skies and prayed to the gods.

Here I Sit Again

Alvin S. Dudley (*Virginia*)

Here I sit again in prison doing time once again and this is my last time of doing time because it is just a waste of time when there are other things in life to do besides doing time.

A Natural?

Glenn Faulkner (*Massachusetts*)

Natural talent in writing . . . is there really such a thing? I am inclined to think not. I mean, where does the flow of thoughts really come from? Can anyone answer me? Come on, answer me.

I sit here day after day and then long into the nights, writing table cleared, the television set off, and my mind open. For what? Frustration! Now that comes quite naturally. I want words—long ones, short ones. I demand profound thoughts and complete ideas . . . magic potions.

The pen is poised. My arm is rigid, my fingers at the ready like so many soldiers. I have only to give my orders and they will write. But alas, no such orders ever come. I fight on alone.

A natural soldier? No . . . a learned warrior. A natural writer? I think not. A frustrated communicator? Yes!

Sunup to Sundown

James Bobbitt (*Virginia*)

I was born in 1927 on a farm in Virginia. I was taken out of the second grade at age 11 to work on the farm. The farm belonged to a white man. It consisted of 50 to 60 acres. I worked six days a week, Monday through Saturday. I started work on the farm at 6 A.M. At 11:30, I was given lunch, and I returned to work at 1 P.M. In the winter, I worked until 5 P.M.; in summer, I worked until 7 P.M.

I started the day by feeding the hogs, chickens, cows and horses. This chore was done before I was given breakfast. After breakfast, I went out in the field. My job was to plow the field with a horse, then plant wheat, rye and oats in September, corn in April and tobacco in May.

The end of June and the month of July, we harvested the wheat, rye and oats. In July, we cleared off the tobacco leaves, starting at the bottom and working up to the top of the plant. The tobacco was then dried in a barn until it was ready for auction in September. In

September we picked the corn. In the winter months, we chopped wood and did the daily chores.

I was paid 25 cents a day plus my meals until I reached age 18. My pay was then increased to $5.00 a week.

After I turned 18, I left the farm and joined the army. I spent 36 weeks in the army. After being discharged, I moved to Connecticut. I got a job in a fur factory making fur hats and coats.

Old Man Time

Anthony Rollins (*Vermont*)

He could be found every morning with tattered clothes and shaking hands, sitting on the park bench, staring at the pigeons. I never once saw him look up. He was always staring at those birds. He seemed to be lost in his own world. I often wondered if I dared step into his world. But I would walk by, afraid I would be sucked into his world if I stopped.

On my way to work one cold November morning, I was sure he wouldn't be there. But there he was, looking sadder and lonelier than ever. I started past him but found myself stopping. I turned and watched him for a moment. His mouth was moving, but I couldn't tell if he was mumbling or shivering from the cold.

I looked at my watch without thinking and found I had 20 minutes before I had to be at work. I slowly took a seat next to him and looked at the pigeons. After watching for a minute, I noticed the pigeons had a certain way of moving that I had never noticed before. They seemed to be dancing around the old man's feet.

I turned to the old man and said, "That's funny. I never noticed the way they move."

He stared at me for a moment, then said in a slow, low voice, "People seldom do, friend." He turned back to the pigeons and I heard him say, "They'll never understand." Then he rose and slowly shuffled off, the birds right behind him.

"Wait," I yelled. "I'd like to talk to you."

Without turning, he said, "You've no time for stories, young man." Then he disappeared down a path.

I sat and stared at the ground a moment. Then, as I looked at my watch, I heard myself say, "He's right." I got up and headed for work.

I never saw that old man again, but I often wondered why I never took the time to talk to him before.

Prison

Michael E. (*New York*)

Prison is a place where a man becomes a
number and has to fight for respect.

Prison is a place where a man becomes strong
mentally or loses touch with reality.

Prison is a place where a man finds himself and
learns how to deal with peer pressure.

Prison is a place where a man decides which
way he's going, negative or positive.

Prison is a place where a man gets wise in
knowledge.

Prison is a place where a man learns to deal
with racism and prejudice and knows what
it is to hate.

Prison is a place where a man begins to see
what's really going on in society.

Prison is a place where a man learns to help
others.

But most of all, prison is a place where no one
should be.

Alone at Last

Pamela Soucy (*Massachusetts*)

Alone at last. All the games of people getting over on one another, the loudness of MTV and, of course, the girl talk. The doors are locked, a time to feel safe and be alone with my thoughts. Time to finally get into bed and fantasize about where I wish to be. Tonight I'd like to take a walk on the beach where it's so quiet. No one in sight. Just the tide splashing against the rocks. Sit on the wharf with my feet in the water, going with the rhythm of the waves. How I miss him. Wish we were together right now. To touch his face. His skin so soft, his eyes the color of the sea, his hair so smooth and his chest so strong. His touch is so gentle and warm. When his arms are around me, I feel so complete, no one or nothing could ever interfere. How I long to hear the words "I love you." The water is getting cold on my feet. Guess it's time to slip under the covers and into the only freedom I know.

Mechanics of the Heart

Ricky Lee Coleman (*Virginia*)

My heart is always in my work when I decide to fix a car. There is no greater feeling to me than when I take an engine apart, find the problem, then fix it. Working with my hands and my mind gives me a great feeling of peace.

You must be totally dedicated to achieving the best results. The work can be hard and dirty but the success of making a sick engine purr can also make your heart soar with pride.

I have worked on cars with my Dad and brothers since an early age. My Dad was always encouraging me and teaching me many things about the mechanics of making a car run with precision.

Many times I've worked alone. During these times, a great feeling of peace and accomplishment stirs within me. It is truly a heartfelt thing when you complete a job well done and an honest day's work.

The Gift

Richard Coursey (*Massachusetts*)

I can still see her sitting in the swing on the front porch of the large white farmhouse. She would swing back and forth in a lazy motion and work on the tasks she could accomplish sitting down—shelling peas, shucking corn, peeling pears or apples, sewing, reading, or just talking and laughing. She laughed so easily, the sound coming from the very center of her soul and infecting those around her. Her belly would jiggle, adding a visual connection to the depths of her joy. She always spoke of joy, peace and love. I can't think of anyone she ever turned away or spoke badly of. She believed in Jesus and her life was one which even the most pious of people might envy. My great-grandmother certainly possessed the love of Christ in her heart.

I spent many summers there playing with my cousins, hunting, fishing and, when I was older, working in the tobacco fields. It was there that I lost my childhood innocence. Through all this, Grandma (everyone called her that, not just her own grandchildren) encouraged and supported me to be a better person, to let God into my life and, most importantly, to "love ever'body," as she put it.

People from the rural farm community knew her and came to the house to talk, laugh and bask in the warm glow of love that emanated from her. In my later years, I learned that she took my mother and me in when I was a baby. My father had abandoned us. When I was about three years old, my father almost killed my mother and me but Grandma stepped in. Not only was she kind and compassionate, she was brave too.

I remember visiting her in the nursing home. Her children, now old themselves, were standing around, and the smell of death was heavy in the air. I had traveled many miles to pay my last respects to this marvelous gift of God while she could still laugh and I could be graced by her presence one last time. She had had a stroke and now could not speak. I stood by the bed and gently took her hand—as she had taken mine so many times—and whispered, "Grandma, it's me. I've come to visit you and let you know I still love you." She looked at me for a moment as recognition came into her eyes. Then she gripped my hand tightly and smiled. I asked if she knew who I was, and she shook her head to say yes. I stood there and carried on a one-sided conversation while those strong hands held mine as if she never wanted to let go.

Her children treated her as if she were just a child and no longer an adult. It was reflected in their tones of voice, actions and auras. I confronted them to no avail. As I drove away from the brick nursing home, I cried. I knew I would never see her alive again. I prayed that her children might be forgiven for robbing her of her last possession, her dignity.

The Tall Fence

Warren Brown (*Virginia*)

Each day is a challenge, behind the tall fence. You try to do whatever it takes to set yourself free from the tall fence. In the morning, you wake up, wash your face, dress, get ready for breakfast, prepare yourself for work, school or trade.

You feel your mind focus on everyday life and wonder if everything will work out so you can be free from the tall fence. Behind all the fences and brick walls, you meet a melting pot of people from all walks of life.

You hope and pray your day will come soon so you can be free from the tall fence. Guards inside and guards looking out from their towers outside make sure you don't try to get through or under the tall fence.

There's nothing like your freedom, so stay out of trouble so the tall fence won't take you from the free world.

Never Taken Alive

Peter A. (*Massachusetts*)

He ran ruthlessly without direction through the
    thickest fields of grazing grasses.
He leaped fiercely over river rocks to the point
    of exhaustion.
He was the last of his kind yet, deep inside, he
    knew he would never be taken alive.

Powerful he was among his tribe that once was.
Now, powerless, hunted by a world which
    would not understand
That this piece of land was his and only his to
    command.

Stubborn Bear was his name and stubborn as a
    bear he would be.
He knew deep inside that he would never be
    taken alive.

Christmas of 1990

James Gaither (*Virginia*)

I spent the Christmas of 1990 in a small town in Virginia. It was a very nice Christmas. My daughter and son and grandchildren spent this special Christmas with me. For, you see, I'm in prison and I might never spend another Christmas with them. This Christmas will be spent alone with only the memories of Christmas past.

A Good-bye Letter to the Drug of My Choice

Darryl T. Woods (*Virginia*)

Dear Cocaine:

Living without you won't be easy. You made me feel as though the world was mine. I so adored and admired you for this. You gave me joy and a great deal of pain.

You never really stayed around that long. When I needed you, you were never there. When you left, my self-esteem went with you. Every time I thought of being with you, I felt anxious and unsure about a moment of happiness that would leave me alone with sadness, guilt and depression.

I was so infatuated with you that I put you before my mother, my sister, my brother, my friends and, most of all, before myself. You were everything to me; you were my life. I will never forget you for the pain I have been through.

As I see it now, we were never meant for each other because we have different goals. My goal is to live up to my potential; yours is to destroy. There is nothing we can offer one another. Whatever you thought you once had for me, you no longer have. You're not good enough for anyone anymore.

Merry Christmas

Jeffrado M. (*Massachusetts*)

By the old stone fireplace in his living room sat Rupert Lewis, whittling a stick as he softly whistled a Christmas carol.

The living room, like the house, was genuinely "Colonial." The only light was from the fireplace. The walls were dazzling orange and red as the fire blazed. Rupert rocked slowly in his antique rocking chair as he whittled. With his spectacles resting on top of his nose and his all-white, shoulder-length hair, Rupert looked like a picture-perfect Saint Nick.

Outside of Rupert's three-room house, a light snow was falling. The marshy ground around the house was frozen so the snow accumulated easily. From somewhere in the nearby forest, a wolf bayed into the dark moonless night.

The howl sent a chill up Rupert's spine. He had never cared for the sound of wolves. He rarely heard them because they had become scarce in the past ten years. He wondered what a wolf could possibly eat now that all the farms in the area had vanished.

The front door of Rupert's little shack exploded inward. The cold came rushing in. As Rupert jumped to his feet, a half-wolf/half-man walked into the room out of the darkness.

Standing fully erect (over six feet tall) and with long sharp teeth, the wolf growled, "Merry Christmas, Rupert. Won't you join me for dinner tonight?"

The wolf slowly advanced toward Rupert. With the quickness of a cat, Rupert stabbed the pointed end of the stick he had been whittling into the wolf's eye. The wolf's cry pierced the night. There was a cloud of blue smoke and—poof—the wolf disappeared.

Missing in Action

James F. McCabe (*Virginia*)

He was twenty when his chopper went down;
They searched for survivors but he wasn't
    found.
He was missing in action and he still is today.
His buddies came back but he had to stay.

He couldn't remember a day without pain.
He lives with the fear of going insane.
His life's like a story that's too sad to tell.
He dreams about heaven, then wakes up in
    hell.

Until he comes home, our country can't rest.
He gave us his all; let's give him our best.
He just keeps hoping he'll get back some day.
He's counting on us; we must find a way.

Missing in action in a land far away,
Feeling forgotten, trying to pray.
Thinking of home, living in fear,
He first counted days, now he counts years.

Wake-Up Call to America

Derrick W. Brooks (*Maryland*)

Another baby has been born with AIDS—who cares? Many people are dying homeless, living on American streets, strung out on drugs—who cares? Unprotected sex among teenagers is on the rise—unimportant, you say.

Then, on November 7, 1991, the mystery and wizardry of Earvin Johnson, Jr., came to an end. He was HIV positive. I, as a fan of Magic Johnson for many years, question the morals of a society in which it takes sports entertainers (who get too, too much attention already) to contract a disease before people begin to pay attention to it. America should be crying out that anyone has to suffer from AIDS.

Like the rest of America, I'm shocked, saddened, frustrated. Scared into caring not only for an American sports legend but for those of lesser status—the babies, the homeless, the teenagers. Wake up, America.

Eddie

O. D. Woods (*Wisconsin*)

My brother Eddie is the sixth of 13 children and much older than me. He looked after me while my mother and father worked in the fields. Eddie took me everywhere he went.

There was a pond in the woods in back of our house. Eddie liked to go swimming, and he would take me to the pond. I would sit and watch Eddie and his friends swim. Whenever I tried to get into the pond, Eddie would make me get out and tell me I was too little to swim.

One day Eddie got an inner tube and pumped it up with air. When we got to the pond, he told me to step into the inner tube and he tied it around my waist. He told me the inner tube would make me stay afloat. We got into the pond and Eddie pushed me into deeper waters. He told me to kick with my feet and paddle with my hands. And that's how Eddie taught me to swim.

Sometimes Eddie and I would go into the woods with our father while he checked his traps. And we would see bears, deer, bobcats, skunks, foxes, vultures, alligators, snakes, squirrels, rabbits and armadillos. And sometimes I would get scared and cry and tell Eddie that the animals might eat me. He would tell me that they were not going to bother me. Eddie never seemed to be scared of going into the woods.

One day we went riding in the woods. The horse threw me and I called Eddie for help. My arm was hurting and I started to cry. He took me to a friend's house. The mother said my arm was broken. Eddie put his hand on my head and told me I would be okay. I looked at Eddie and he was crying. I had never seen Eddie get scared or cry about anything. I asked him why he was crying. He said because I had hurt myself. After that, Eddie stopped taking me into the woods. He even stopped swimming or riding. Most of the time, we sat on the porch swing and talked.

In 1986, Eddie had to be operated on twice. I took off from my job to go see him. When Eddie's wife and I got to the hospital room, he was unconscious. I sat there telling Eddie's wife about the things we did as children. When Eddie regained consciousness, we talked and joked about each other.

My Companion

Moana (*Massachusetts*)

Four months pregnant, wearing the dress I'd worn to court—the dress that was meant to elicit sympathy from the sentencing judge, but which had failed miserably—I was handcuffed in front and led into a long building with screened windows.

Rather than having impressed the judge with the fact that I'd returned from Florida to face my legal troubles clean and sober and pregnant, I had stood before him and felt the power of his disgust and hatred for me as he insured I would be incarcerated past the date I was due to deliver my second child.

As I was led down the long corridor, wooden doors on either side, I heard the sounds of too many women in too small an area. A door was opened for me and I walked into a cell designed to hold two women. In it were three bunk beds lining the walls, and five women, all sitting or lying on their beds, for lack of floor space. A toilet stood opposite the beds, and a sink behind that. A three-drawer bureau was meant to hold the belongings of the six women in the room.

The empty bed was on top of the middle bunk; the gray-colored sheets and torn blanket were folded on the thin mattress. After I haphazardly made the bed, I crawled up into the bunk and sat cross-legged, smoking a cigarette. I could feel the heat radiating down from the ceiling and was soon covered with sweat.

During my stay in this medical holding unit, I saw and felt the powerlessness of the women forced to endure this filthy, inhumane treatment. Sadly, rather than working together to effect some kind of change in the conditions forced upon us, the women split into warring factions, causing each other more pain than the institution itself subjected us to.

At night, when I restlessly tried to sleep, I would feel the baby moving within me, and I would be grateful he was in there safe and warm. I'd communicate silently with him. He was my companion during this awful period in my life. When I looked into his newborn face, I felt as though I'd known him a very long time.

Labrador

Leonard L. Daigneault (*Massachusetts*)

Shining black coat sleek

Deep brown trusting eyes full of love

A shapely head containing a drooling, lolling tongue

Looking at me expectantly, waiting as if to say, what is next, my lord and master

Silent he is but every move is alive and telling me over and over I love you, I trust you—let's play

Putting his huge head on my knees looking at me again expectantly, waiting wagging his sturdy tail

I smile from all this for the small pleasures thus given

Perhaps an idiot could do the same things except for the tail-wagging part

Thump! he throws himself down his breath in short pants

Head on top of his sturdy legs lying there waiting

He cocks me an eye, wary at the passing of a belligerent cat

Then closes his eyes and snores asleep just like that

Leaving Vietnam

Long Van Vo (*Virginia*)

I was just a young kid growing up in Vietnam. What I liked the most was being able to see my mother every day. I never wanted to live without my parents and sisters.

Life was hard for us in Vietnam so my family decided to send me to America. I still remember the night I last saw my mother. I was standing in front of her and I couldn't think of anything to say at the time. My mother was very upset also. She said, "Take care of yourself, my son." I was really upset because I didn't want to leave my family behind.

I was put aboard a small, frail ship and I watched as my home slowly disappeared. I haven't seen any of my family since, and I miss them so much. I try to write to them as often as I can.

I'm living in America now, and I want so much to make something of myself so I can afford to send for my family. One of these days, I'm going to be with my family again, right here in America.

Angels with Broken Wings

Ronald Deaver (*Virginia*)

They live in the deepest part of their emotions.
They hide in the farthest parts of their minds.
They try each day to escape, but
The abuse continues to leave them blind.

When you look at them, you will see
The fear and confusion in their eyes.
When you talk with them, you will hear
The pain and suffering in their precious little
lives.

So remember, when you try to show them love
and affection
And they turn quickly and distance themselves
from you,
Don't feel offended.

Love is just something that an abused child is
not used to.

Don't Be Used, Stay in School

William Armstrong (*Virginia*)

When I was a 17-year-old dropout, I was a construction worker with a private contractor. I worked in the rain, snow, sleet and all kinds of weather. I always worked a 40- to 50-hour week. When it came time to be paid, the paycheck was always eight to ten hours short. Unable to read or write, I had no way of proving my hours. I was being cheated and could do nothing about it. After a couple of years of abuse, I used my memory and work experience to work on my own. When guys worked for me, I treated them fairly. Everyone except one person thought I could read and write. I was very good at bluffing and charming my workers. Since my incarceration, I've learned to read and write. When I'm released, I won't have to bluff anymore but I can still be just as charming as I was before.

To My Son

Larry J. H. (*Virginia*)

Dear Son:

This is a special writing for you to help you understand why we cannot be together. At times you may feel angry at me and think that if I really loved you, I wouldn't have left you. I would have stayed at home.

So I want you to understand that I had to go away. I broke the law and that means that I did something I shouldn't have done. I had to go to court, and the judge sent me to a special place called a correctional institution for men.

This place is not like the jails they show on TV. We do have guards here but they do not carry guns.

All the men here live on a schedule, just as you do at home. We eat together in a big room like the cafeteria in a school. The food is okay. Every day, everyone goes to school or has a job to do. At night, we can watch TV. The hardest part for me is that I cannot be with you.

Some kids think that if they had been better children, their fathers would have stayed at home. But this isn't true. You had nothing to do with the reason I had to come here. And there was nothing you could have done to change what happened to me. I'm here because of my own problems.

One father told me his child tried to get into trouble too, so he'd be sent here to be with him. But children cannot stay here and it made him sad to have his child get into trouble.

While I have to be away, I trust that you will do your best to get along well at school, at home and in the neighborhood. I want you to have a good life now and in the future. Remember that the people taking care of you are doing it for you and me.

Someday I hope that you and I will talk about what happened to me, and how you felt and what you did while we had to be apart.

For now, let's be brave and strong. Please carry my love with you always.

Your father

Doing Time

Dexter Beattie (*Massachusetts*)

Time is the invisible enemy of incarceration. Time is slip-sliding away like tiny grains of pure white sand falling freely through an hourglass. That's how we see our lives passing before us. An indifferent, cruel aging—time we can't have back. Yesterday's a cancelled check, tomorrow's a promissory note, today is the cash in hand. To live in the moment is all we can do. To live one day at a time brings true meaning to being incarcerated.

Incarceration can be a strange blessing, a chance to end life's ridiculous, never-ending tape of the past playing in our heads. Had we not been thrown off the merry-go-round of life, we might be dead. For some, prison is the savior from death. Incarceration is an opportunity to reflect, make better choices and find a new direction at the crossroads. It's a time to empty out the attic of old habits, thoughts and fears. It's a time to fill the empty space with new, exciting and sometimes scary thoughts.

All this has come true for me. I discovered a

new friend whom I love very much—me. I thought of all the years I have wasted. I never had the pleasure of discovering who I really am.

Now I spend time learning all about me. This experience is wonderful, exciting and sometimes very painful. It's a chance to grow, find peace and calmness, a love I never knew before.

They may lock up my body but not my mind. I am free inside.

Montreal: Spirited Heart of French Canada

Dean (*Massachusetts*)

It is a blue and white day in Montreal, the colors of a summer sky and the flag of the province of Quebec. On the sidewalks of Rue Sherbrooke flutter thousands of the flags, a white fleur-de-lis on an azure background, the symbol of New France. Thousands of people have come to honor the patron saint of French Quebec, St. Jean-Baptiste—John the Baptist.

"You Americans have your Fourth of July," a bystander tells me. "English Canadians celebrate on July first. June 24 is our day—this day is French."

The crowd is frisky with the first warm weather after a rainy spring. It is the biggest St. Jean-Baptiste parade since 1968. That year French-speaking separatists threw bottles and tomatoes at Pierre Trudeau, then the nation's prime minister and a French Quebecer who stood for Canadian unity. Today there is no hint of violence but emotion is palpable. It hovers like heat shimmers as speeches ring out across the park that hosted the 1976 Olympics.

"There is a place for us and that is here," one speaker says. "There is a language for us and that is French. There is a time for us and that is now!" The flags wave.

The Invincible Wall

Richard Lawrence Kraemer (*Wisconsin*)

You kick and punch,
Push and pull,
Cry and mope,
Rebel and fight,
You even try smiling.
But nothing moves the invincible wall.

Drink and My Favorite Car

Richard L. Abbitt (*Virginia*)

When I was in high school, I always wanted to drag race and drive fast cars. In my ninth-grade year, I took a '70 Nova and built it from the ground up.

When I got out of high school, my dreams came true. My grass green Nova was ready for the track. I won all the races that year. No one could understand how a short man like me could drive a big car like that.

The next year, I decided to go to the track to drink. After the drinks, my friend and I decided to race my car. I totaled my car and my best friend. I got seriously hurt too.

The next time I went to the track, everyone wanted to know how such a short man could drive such a big wheelchair! Fast cars and drinks are not a good mix. It will only get you in a four wheel car without a motor.

Man/Woman

Rose Mary L. (*Ohio*)

They are so hard to understand.
One day they are by your side,
The next they gone.
It don't matter how many men you be with,
They all the same.
They all get fancy cars.
They all say they love you.
Half of them don't even know what love is.
Some got children, some don't.
It don't matter because Man is Man.
I wish I had a dollar for every time
They say I love you and don't mean it.

They are so easy to get hurt.
But they love a man with all their heart
And get hurt anyway.
I will never know why
They even put their self through that.
They are so easy to get hurt
But they keep trying.
Most of all, women are kind.
They say they sorry
When they know that they did nothing.
One day they will learn not to fall so deep in
    love.
But until then, Woman will just be Woman.

My Vision

Dartinerro Robin Clark (*Wisconsin*)

I dreamed I was in heaven. Everybody had a special gift. Mine was singing. I sang low but clear and very proud.

The Lord used to come around to hear me sing. I never saw God. He was a spirit like I was. When he came on the scene, everyone felt his powerful and unique love. His love was so filling, you could never be jealous about sharing his love with everybody.

I was asked to sing for the Lord because he was upset about what was happening on earth. He was selecting people from heaven to come down to spread his gospel and his love. I wanted so very much to do his will that I asked him if I could go. I could feel he was a little hurt by my asking but he let me go. He told me to watch out for Satan. I felt a little insecure and asked the Lord, "Will I do all right? Are you going to watch over me?" I sensed he was angry when he said, "Don't you have faith?"

The message he told us to spread is that no matter how mischievous you are, you can always come to him.

Thank You

Larry J. H. (*Virginia*)

Thank you for every thought, act and word of love, even when I may not have deserved it.

Thank you for the time out of your life that you could have spent it elsewhere.

Thank you for never disappointing me, even when your life would have been easier if you had.

Thank you for making me feel and know I was the most beautiful person in the world, even at times when I didn't feel it.

Thank you for sharing the hard times in my life, even when yours may have been harder and your responsibilities greater.

Thank you for loving me, even enough at times to let me go my own way.

And thank you for letting me return to you and for letting me know that I was always meant to be yours.

Going Home

Curtis N. (*Virginia*)

I just made parole after being in prison for four years. I don't like being in here, but I keep coming back because I drink and use drugs. I don't want to come back here, so I'm doing the things that will help me out in the world today and for years to come.

Going back out there scares me a lot. Last year, a friend of mine from here got out and I just heard he was killed. Another guy who went home recently killed himself. Guys leave here with good intentions and high hopes. But sometimes the pressure gets too much for them and they fall back to doing things they said they wouldn't do anymore—or they just give up.

I was a mean person out there so I don't know what's going to happen to me. Leaving here is good but not knowing what's going to happen is bad. The streets are what you make them, the same way as in here. I hope that what I've learned in here will help me make it on the street.

Advice to Writers

from the creative writing class at
Hampshire House of Correction,
Northampton, Massachusetts

Come in,
sit down,
listen,
have fun,
write anything,
write for yourself.
Take the advice given as a friendly gesture.
Make time to do your own creative writing.
Practice,
practice,
practice.

Dexter Beattie

Try to relax,
meditate
and let your imagination run wild.

John Lefas

Come with an open mind,
concerning all the different facets of the writing
    field, and utilize both the pros and cons of
    each in the field you choose.
Write what draws you most
in the way of expressing yourself.

Eric P. Yetton

❖

Try and relax, don't force it.
Listen and hear your inner voice,
try and think of a beginning,
middle
and an ending.
Have faith in yourself,
believe in you. . . .

Glenn Faulkner

❖

Hey Dude, just write.
Take it easy man;
and like try and do the assignments.

Jeffrado M.

I Sometimes Wonder

Stephon T. B. (*Virginia*)

I sometimes wonder if I will be like a trained bird when it is set free.

Or will I be that one in a million and go on with my life and not return?

To Our Readers

We hope to publish more anthologies like this one. But to do that, we need writing by you, our readers. If you are enrolled in an adult basic skills program or an ESOL program, we would like to see your writing. If you have a piece of writing you would like us to consider for a future book, please send it to us. It can be on any subject; it can be a true story, fiction or poetry. We can't promise that we will publish your story but we will give it serious consideration. We will let you know what our decision is.

Please do not send us your original manuscript. Instead, make a copy of it and send that to us, because we can't promise that we will be able to return it to you.

If you send us your writing, we will assume you are willing for us to publish it. If we decide to accept it, we will send a letter requesting your permission. So please be sure to include your name, address and phone number on the copy you send us.

We look forward to seeing your writing.

The Editors
Literacy Volunteers of New York City
121 Sixth Avenue, New York, NY 10013

Three series of good books for all readers:

Writers' Voices—A multicultural, whole-language series of books offering selections from some of America's finest writers, along with background information, maps, glossaries, questions and activities and many more supplementary materials for readers. Our list of authors includes: Amy Tan • Alex Haley • Alice Walker • Rudolfo Anaya • Louise Erdrich • Oscar Hijuelos • Maxine Hong Kingston • Gloria Naylor • Anne Tyler • Tom Wolfe • Mario Puzo • Avery Corman • Judith Krantz • Larry McMurtry • Mary Higgins Clark • Stephen King • Peter Benchley • Ray Bradbury • Sidney Sheldon • Maya Angelou • Jane Goodall • Mark Mathabane • Loretta Lynn • Katherine Jackson • Carol Burnett • Kareem Abdul-Jabbar • Ted Williams • Ahmad Rashad • Abigail Van Buren • Priscilla Presley • Paul Monette • Robert Fulghum • Bill Cosby • Lucille Clifton • Robert Bly • Robert Frost • Nikki Giovanni • Langston Hughes • Joy Harjo • Edna St. Vincent Millay • William Carlos Williams • Terrence McNally • Jules Feiffer • Alfred Uhry • Horton Foote • Marsha Norman • Lynne Alvarez • Lonne Elder III • ntozake shange • Neil Simon • August Wilson • Harvey Fierstein • Beth Henley • David Mamet • Arthur Miller and Spike Lee.

New Writers' Voices—A series of anthologies and individual narratives by talented new writers. Stories, poems and true life experiences written by adult learners cover such topics as health, home and family, love, work, facing challenges and life in foreign countries. Many *New Writers' Voices* contain photographs and illustrations.

Reference—A reference library for adult new readers and writers. The first two books in the series are *How to Write a Play* and *Discovering Words: The Stories Behind English.*

Write for our free complete catalog:
LVNYC Publishing Program
121 Avenue of the Americas
New York, New York 10013